THE MAGIC AMBER

For my wife Teri, who keeps my rice pot full.
– C. R.

Library of Congress Cataloging-in-Publication Data

Reasoner, Charles.
      The magic amber / retold & illustrated by Charles Reasoner.
            p.   cm.—(Legends of the world)
      Summary: An old rice farmer and his wife are repaid for their
kindness and generosity.
      ISBN 0-8167-3407-0 (library)   ISBN 0-8167-3408-9 (pbk.)
      [1. Folklore--Korea.]   I. Title.   II. Series.
398.21—dc20
[E]   93-43180

THE MAGIC AMBER

A KOREAN LEGEND

RETOLD AND ILLUSTRATED BY CHARLES REASONER

TROLL ASSOCIATES

A long time ago, in a simple farmhouse in Korea, there lived a kindly old rice farmer and his wife. The couple was so poor they had barely enough food to keep themselves alive. What little rice they had was given as payment for all their hard work in the fields of their landlord, Lon Po.

One day the old farmer and his wife found that their supply of rice had dwindled to a mere handful.

"Alas, we will starve this winter," cried the wife.

"Let us not think about misfortune," the husband replied as he set the rice pot over a small cracking fire.

While the winter winds howled, the warm aroma of cooking rice

filled the hut. At last, when the rice was cooked, the husband placed bowls and chopsticks on the table. But just as he and his wife were about to begin their meal, there came a soft tapping at the door.

The old man needed all his strength to keep the fierce winds from blowing open the door. Slowly, a shivering snow-covered figure entered the couple's home. It was an old woman, blue with cold.

am sor-ry t-to both-ther y-you," the old woman stammered as she sat down on a straw mat.

"It is no trouble, stranger," the old man said as he wrapped her trembling shoulders in a warm blanket. "You must be hungry. We have little to eat. But what little we have we will share with you."

At once the stranger dipped into the pot and began to eat the rice. She ate so quickly that, before the couple could stop her, the rice was all gone. Satisfied, the stranger rose to her feet and bowed deeply to her generous hosts.

"Thank you," the old woman said. "You have given me strength to continue on my journey. Now I must repay you for your kindness." With that, she took a brightly colored amber stone from a small pouch at her side and placed it in the old man's hands.

"Many blessings on your house," said the old woman. She closed the door behind her and was swallowed up by the night.

"A stone!" cried the wife. "Oh, my husband, we cannot eat a stone. We will surely starve now!"

As the old man tossed the stone into the rice pot, its hollow sound reminded him of the ache in his own empty belly. "Let us not think only of our stomachs," said the husband. "At least we have a house to keep us warm. Tomorrow I will ask Lon Po if he can spare a little more rice for us. Now come along, my old and faithful wife. Let us rest."

The next morning the road to Lon Po's house was covered with snow from the stormy night. At last the old man stood before the gate of Lon Po's house. A servant brought him to the breakfast table. The old man's stomach churned as he saw all the food. Yet he bowed humbly and made his simple request for a small bag of rice.

"So, you wish to have even more rice," said Lon Po as he sipped his tea. "Perhaps your wife is wasting food and that is why you are without! But I am a generous man. I will give you a bag of rice. But you must repay me with three bags from the next harvest."

"You are most kind, Lon Po," said the old man. "It shall be as you say." And he hurried home through the snow, holding onto the rice bag tightly.

A small fire warmed the hut as the old man brought forth the bag of rice and told his wife the price of Lon Po's kindness.

"Three bags! How can we ever repay him when we barely have enough to feed ourselves?" cried the old woman.

"Wife, we must be thankful that we have enough food for the winter," said the old farmer. "Besides, I'm sure you will think differently when your stomach is full."

The old man stirred the embers of the fire and added a few sticks of wood to make a small blaze. His wife went to lift the rice pot and fill it with water.

"Oh, my husband," groaned the old woman, "I must be weak from hunger. This rice pot is too heavy for me to move."

"I, too, must be weak," gasped the old man as he tried to lift the pot.

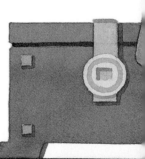

Together, the old couple sat on the floor with their little rice pot and lifted the lid to peek inside. To their amazement, the pot was brimming with rice! As they poured out the rice, the amber stone tumbled out. The old man looked curiously at the amber and placed it back into the rice pot. Again, the pot was filled with rice! Three times the old man placed the stone into the pot. And three times the pot was filled to overflowing.

"We have been blessed!" the old man exclaimed.

Not only did the couple eat well that day, but for the remainder of that winter as well. In time, they began to sell the rice that the magic amber provided and became prosperous. Their rice was known as the best-tasting in all the land.

Even with their new wealth, the couple remembered their days of hunger and always gave to those in need. They would take bags of rice to the families of village fishermen whose nets came up empty. A bag of rice would quietly be given to a woodcutter's family when he became ill. Everyone in the village knew who had brought the gift.

The old couple was respected and honored for their generosity. Occasionally, a fisherman would bring them a fine fish in gratitude, or a basket of fresh vegetables would appear on their doorstep. The old couple accepted these gifts with quiet smiles and never turned away anyone in need.

oon, news of the couple's good fortune spread far and wide. Eventually, it reached the ears of Lon Po.

"So, it would seem that the old rice farmer's luck has changed," said Lon Po. "Perhaps it is time to pay the old man a visit and collect on a debt."

With long strides, Lon Po came to the house of the old farmer and his wife and pounded on the door. "I demand the three bags of rice that you owe me from last winter!" he shouted.

"Honorable Lon Po," said the old man, "although our agreement was to repay you from the next harvest, it shall be as you wish. Please come and rest from your long journey, and I will pay you what I owe."

"Very well," said Lon Po. "I will have some of your tea while you fill my three rice bags."

The old man began to fill Lon Po's rice bags while his wife prepared a pot of ginseng tea. Lon Po watched as the old man took a shiny amber stone from a hidden shelf and dropped it into an old rice pot. To his amazement, the pot filled with rice and the old man filled Lon Po's rice bags to overflowing.

"Ho! So that is the old man's secret!" thought Lon Po. He gathered his three rice bags and excused himself hurriedly, leaving the old couple with their pot of ginseng tea.

The very next day, a ragged beggar came to the old couple's door.

"Perhaps I might do some small tasks around your home in exchange for a bowl of rice," he said.

Not wanting to rob him of his dignity, the couple allowed the beggar to sweep the few rice kernels from their back room after he had eaten. When the last speck of rice was picked up, the beggar reappeared and thanked the old couple for their kindness. Then he disappeared as mysteriously as he had arrived.

The next time the old man went to his rice pot, all he found was the amber stone rattling around in the bottom! Again he placed the stone into the pot. Again the pot remained empty.

"Wife! Wife! Something is wrong!" he cried. "The stone has lost its magic! The gods must be angry with us!"

The old woman took the amber in her hand and studied it.

"This is not our magic amber," she said at last. "It is darker in color and has many impurities. Someone has stolen our magic amber and replaced it with this ordinary stone."

The couple stared at each other. "The beggar!" they exclaimed.

Meanwhile, at the edge of a village, near a wide river that flowed to the sea, Lon Po quickly removed the ragged beggar's clothes he was wearing. "Enough of this!" he said impatiently as he stuffed the rags into the hollow of a nearby tree. "With this amber stone, I shall become the wealthiest man in the country." He looked hungrily at the gleaming stone in his hand, then thrust it into his pocket and started across the river in a narrow wooden boat.

But Lon Po had never paddled a boat before. He struggled against the current turning the boat this way and that. Suddenly, the boat went one way while Lon Po went the other.

The river was strong, and Lon Po was swept downstream as he struggled for shore. At last he was able to pull himself onto the river bank, coughing and sputtering.

"At least, I'm still alive and rich," he said to himself as he reached into his pocket for the amber stone. But the stone was gone, swallowed up by the river whose waters flowed to the sea. Lon Po lay on the muddy bank of the river and wept bitter tears.

With the amber stone gone and their supply of rice dwindling, the old couple was once more forced to work in the fields. The labor seemed twice as hard, for their bodies creaked with age.

But the people in the village never forgot the old couple's generosity. They continued to bring them fresh fish and baskets of their finest vegetables. Still the old couple missed the charmed days they had once shared with others.

One day a fisherman left a large catfish for their dinner.

"The people have been so kind to us in our old age," said the old woman as she laid the fish out to clean. "I wish there was a way that we could bless them as we once did."

"You are right, cherished wife," said the man. "But we should be thankful that this fine catfish will be joining us for dinner!"

Just then, the old woman's knife struck something in the belly of the fish. "What is this?" she said as she pulled out a hard round object. And there in her hand was a shiny amber stone—the kind that a fish might pick up from the bottom of a river that flowed to the sea.

 The story of *The Magic Amber* comes from Korea, an ancient country that has been torn by wars for thousands of years. Korea's name itself comes from the word *Koryo*, a name given by one of the many generals that controlled the country. Although the Korean people share a common language, their land is divided into North Korea *(Choson)* and South Korea *(Taehan)*. The Korean peninsula is mountainous, and the country has been an agricultural and fishing one for about 30,000 years. The people produce crops such as rice, soybeans, and millet, and they catch various types of shellfish, pollack, and squid.

Korea is a melting pot of various cultural influences, having been occupied at various times by the Chinese and Japanese. Poor families, such as those in our story, farmed under generals and warlords, and they were forced to pay tribute for protection. Not all of these generals were cruel. Some did build schools and provide books.

Since ancient times, amber has been an object of value and mystery. Although it looks and feels like a stone, amber is actually fossilized, or hardened, sap. The sap comes from a certain variety of pine tree that grew millions of years ago. This fossilized resin sometimes contains air bubbles or ancient insects that became trapped in the sticky substance. Part of the mystery of amber is its ability to become electrically charged when rubbed with a soft cloth. With amber's unusual qualities, it is easy to see why it would play a central part in a story such as *The Magic Amber.*